For Noah, Milo, Zen, and Lotus, and for my mom, Katharyn, and my sister, Nefeterius, and for Iris Peynado —T.P.

For Francesca, Lorenzo, and Mom —F.F.

Farrar Straus Giroux Books for Young Readers
An imprint of Macmillan Publishing Group, LLC
120 Broadway, New York, NY 10271

Text copyright © 2019 by Tamara Pizzoli
Pictures copyright © 2019 by Federico Fabiani
All rights reserved
Color separations by Embassy Graphics
Printed in China by Hung Hing Off-set Printing Co. Ltd., Heshan City, Guangdong Province
Designed by Monique Sterling
Previous edition published by the English School House
First Farrar Straus Giroux edition, 2019
1 3 5 7 9 10 8 6 4 2

mackids.com

Library of Congress Cataloging-in-Publication Data

Names: Pizzoli, Tamara, author. | Fabiani, Federico, illustrator.
Title: Tallulah the Tooth Fairy CEO / Dr. Tamara Pizzoli ; pictures by
  Federico Fabiani.
Description: First Farrar Straus Giroux edition. | New York : Farrar Straus
  Giroux, 2019. | Originally published in Texas by The English Schoolhouse
  in 2016. | Summary: Tallulah the Tooth Fairy, a black businesswoman who
  runs one of the most successful tooth collecting organizations in the
  world, finds herself unexpectedly stumped when six-year-old Ballard
  Burchell leaves a note instead of his tooth under his pillow.
Identifiers: LCCN 2018035810 | ISBN 9780374309190 (hardcover)
Subjects: | CYAC: Tooth Fairy--Fiction. | Business enterprises--Fiction. |
  African Americans--Fiction.
Classification: LCC PZ7.P68985 Tal 2019 | DDC [E]--dc23
LC record available at https://lccn.loc.gov/2018035810

Our books may be purchased in bulk for promotional, educational, or business use.
Please contact your local bookseller or the Macmillan Corporate and Premium Sales Department
at (800) 221-7945 ext. 5442 or by email at MacmillanSpecialMarkets@macmillan.com.

·TALLULAH·
THE TOOTH FAIRY CEO

Dr. Tamara Pizzoli

Pictures by **Federico Fabiani**

FARRAR STRAUS GIROUX

New York

Tallulah the tooth fairy has been in the tooth business for as long as she can remember. She truly loves her work. That's because looking after children's pearly whites is more than just Tallulah's job. It is her career.

Tallulah's passion for teeth led her to start a company called Teeth Titans Incorporated. Now it's the largest tooth-collection organization on the planet, and she is the CEO, or chief executive officer. Later, she founded the National Association for the Appreciation and Care of Primary Teeth—also known as the NAACP-T.

Tuesday and Thursday mornings are
dedicated to yoga, Pilates, and errands.

The Mouth
1970, Toothsie
Lipstick and gummy
worms

Still Life with
Denture
1961, unknown artist
Oil on canvas

This is not a toothbrush.

The Treachery
of Oral Hygiene
1928, Magreeth
Wood and horsehair

Friday mornings are for visiting museums. She finds exhibitions about teeth to be particularly fascinating.

Each afternoon is dedicated to training other tooth fairies.

What? You're not surprised, are you?

Well, *of course* there's more than one tooth fairy.

There are way too many lost teeth in the world for just one fairy to manage. Tallulah is a tooth fairy, after all. She's not Santa Claus—though she *did* once have lunch with Santa's lovely wife, Charlene.

"I just became swamped with all the work, so I had to hire additional fairies. Sure, I'm in it for the teeth; I'd be lying if I said I wasn't. But the greatest satisfaction is knowing that I'm providing a service to children around the world. Each and every fairy is trained by me. I oversee all the hiring . . ."

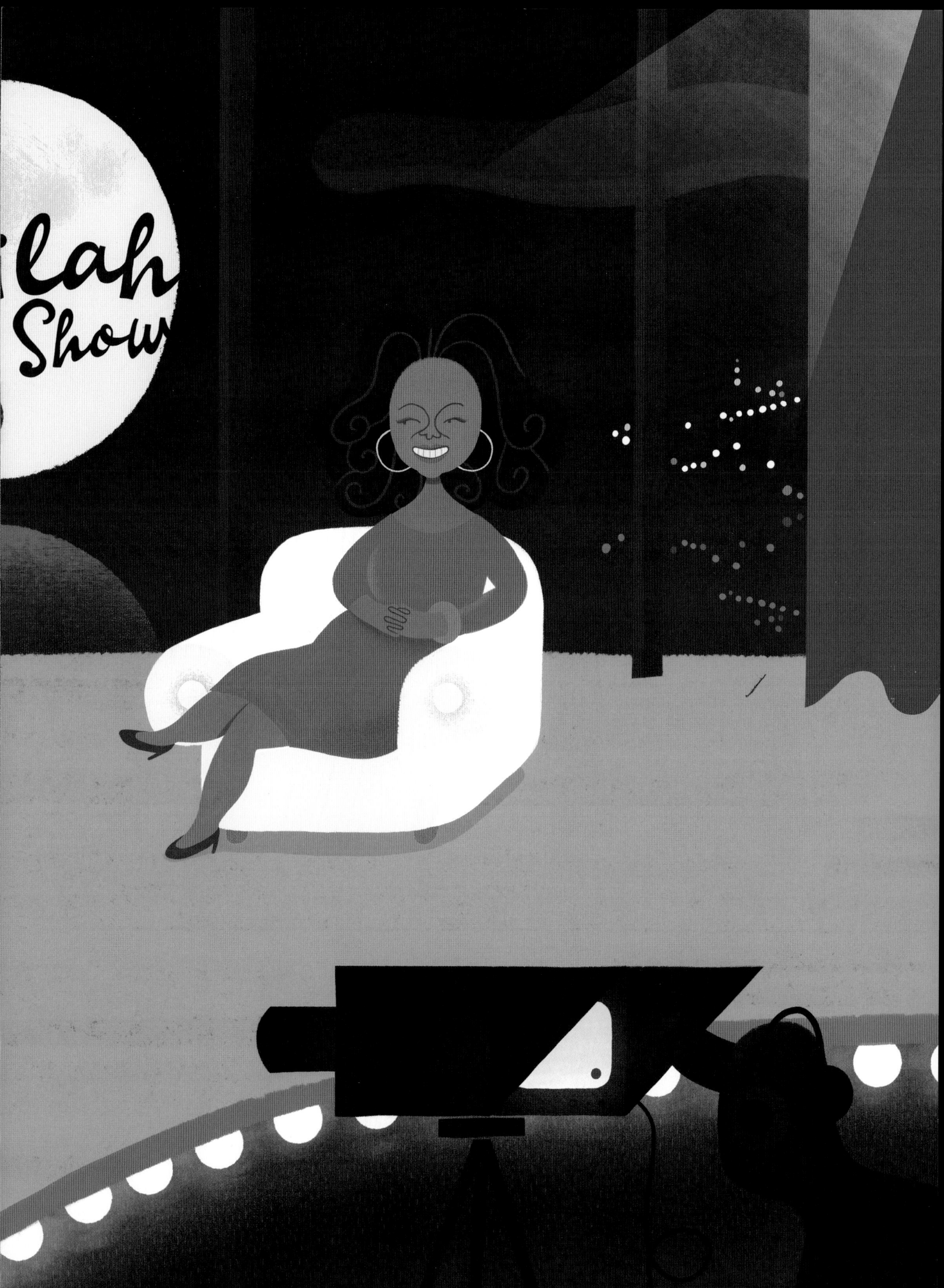
ilah
Show

TOOTH FAIRY
RECRUITMENT EVENT

QUESTIONS YOU MAY GET,
BUT ARE NOT OBLIGATED TO ANSWER

HOW DOES THE TOOTH FAIRY GET IN THE HOUSE?

WHAT DO YOU DO WITH THE TEETH?

HOW ARE YOU NOTIFIED WHEN A TOOTH IS LOST?

With such an effective recruiting strategy, prospective tooth fairies sign up in droves.

Each evening, after an early dinner and a bit of relaxing, Tallulah begins her rounds as head tooth fairy. Sure, she could afford to sit around counting teeth and money, but nothing gives Tallulah quite the same thrill as sliding a shiny tooth out from under a child's pillow and inserting something gleaming and jingly or crisp and easily folded in exchange.

So that's just what she does.
Night after night.
Most nights are pretty routine,
but not all of them.

One evening, something unusual occurred.

Tallulah had gone about her routine and was prepared to make her last stop, at the home of Ballard Burchell.

~~Noah Pizzoli~~
~~Milo Pizzoli~~
~~Zen Pizzoli~~
~~Lotus Pizzoli~~
~~Nefeterius McPherson~~
~~Tiffany Isaacs~~
~~Cicely Jones~~
~~Sae Bom Kim~~
~~Mirabel Obregara~~
~~Lorenzo Fabiani~~
Ballard Burchell

When she slid her hand underneath the boy's pillow, what she found was not at all a treasure of a tooth, but a note written by the boy himself.

Tallulah the tooth fairy studied the note for a moment, then stated, "This looks nothing like me. Why do they always make me so . . . tiny?"

As it was her first time finding a note in place of a tooth, Tallulah pulled out her Teeth Titans Incorporated Employee Manual for reference, but she quickly remembered there was no information pertaining to what to do in case of a lost tooth— not just a wiggly tooth that fell out, but a tooth that was truly *lost*. Though she'd written the manual herself, Tallulah hadn't made provisions for such a rare occurrence.

She had a decision to make. And quick!

Tallulah called an emergency meeting with her board of directors. These seven tooth fairies were the best of the best in her company. She could rely on them for sound advice and direction on how to best address the dilemma.

"In all my years as a professional tooth fairy," Tallulah began, "I have never had this occur. I'm truly stumped and would like your thoughts."

A lengthy discussion ensued.

Late that night, once Tallulah had listened to all the opinions given and reached a decision, she returned to Ballard's bedside to leave him a note of her own—and a little something extra.

TEETH TITANS INC.

Dear Ballard,

Everyone misplaces things sometimes. Here's hoping you find your tooth. Next time, store your lost tooth in this patented Teeth Titans Incorporated tooth compartment lanyard. It retails for $9.95 and is available on my website, but this one is my gift to you.

See you soon,
Tallulah, the Tooth Fairy CEO

The Tooth Fairy

"Mom!" called Ballard. "You'll never believe this!"

He hopped out of bed and ran to his mother to show her both the letter and the photo of the tooth fairy.

And inside the Teeth Titans Incorporated tooth compartment lanyard was one more surprise from Tallulah the Tooth Fairy CEO: the shiniest gold coin you ever did see.